MW01264287

Purrlock Holmes
and the case of
The Vanishing Valuables

Purrlock Holmes
and the case of
The Vanishing Valuables

A paws-on tale of mystery by
Betty Sleep

Cover Illustration- Alma Borcuk
Story Illustrations- Andrew Carruthers, Nikki Doherty
and Alma Borcuk

Copyright © 2004 Betty Sleep

All rights reserved. Printed in the United States of America.
No part of this publication may be reproduced, stored in a retrieval system, or transmitted, in any form
or by any means electronic, mechanical, photocopying, recording, or otherwise, without the prior
written permission of the author.

ISBN: 978-0-9811194-0-3

Published by Felinity Publishing
New Brunswick, Canada

To-

The animals who have brought love, and joy to my life. With special kudos to the inspiration for the main character, the "real" Purrlock Holmes. And to my father, the late Arthur Ash, who taught me as a child, that to laugh is a wonderful thing.

Contents

Acknowledgements

For their unstinting help, Purrlock and Watson are eternally grateful to Wendy Lamirande for her layout expertise, and to Tom Schultz for his endless supply of patience and encouragement to re-release this first book in the Purrlock Holmes series.

A debt of thanks is also owed to our many friends in the cat world, who are fans of both Purrlocks, the real and the fictional- Cathy, Janine, Nancy, Jan & Softail, Carolyn & John, your support is priceless. To the young cat fanciers who reviewed this first volume -a big thank you for a job well done.

We are also grateful for the talents of Andrew Carruthers, illustrator, and Alma Borcuk artist, who created the real image of Purrlock and Watson on the cover. With a tip of the deerstalker hat to Nikki Doherty, for her help with the back cover photo.

This book would never have been written without having lived with and learned to love, the foibles of our animal friends.

[Note to the Editor]

Okay, I don't know who got hold of my password and managed to crack my secret files on Mr. R.'s computer, but there is dog slobber on the keyboard. We'll deal with you later, Mr. Enormous Ears.

For now, let me just say that everything good about me is true, and all the stuff that makes me look bad, was made up by the dog.

Purrlock Holmes, P.I.
(Pretty Inquisitive)

Chapter One

The Game's Afoot

"Did not!"

"Did *too*!"

"Mommmmmmmmmmm!"

And good morning to you too, kids. Geez, they're at it already, and it can't be more than half-past my midnight snack, or a quarter to breakfast. Stevie's got under Rebecca's skin already. I suppose I could make the effort to crawl out from under the blankets, but I like the way Becca leaves them piled up like this. Day after day, after day. I remember reading somewhere that teenagers never make their beds. That's awfully nice of them. I must thank Becca sometime. It's warm, and I can always nap here, when the humans are looking for the dreaded Hairball Hacker, whoever that may be.

Yep, there they go. The *clump-clump* noise on the stairs is Stevie, and from the slap-slap of bare feet, I estimate he's about 2.5 seconds ahead of being thumped by Becca.

Wait…there's a *click-click* bringing up the rear. Darn. If that dog is on the move it must be breakfast time. Guess I have to get up after all. But it's just not cool to arrive exactly at mealtime, or they'll think I'm over eager, and start feeding me that slop in the can, again. You know, the one that has the fat cat with the stupid grin on his face. Like he expects all us lesser feline beings to chow the stuff down, because he recommends it. The guy is making mega bucks from having his kisser on that label, and eats nothing but minced beef, while we get pureed chicken feet.

Oh no! The rolling thump, bump, bang, crash, can only mean one thing. The dog fell down the stairs...again.

I raced out into the hallway. Sure enough, there he was in a pitiful pile of brown and white fur at the foot of the stairs, with Becca bending over him making coo-coo noises, and him giving her the big, brown eyes, and little whimpers. Honestly, it's enough to make me throw up the Twinkies I found hidden under Stevie's bed. I would, too, but I don't see an empty pair of shoes, and one doesn't do that kind of thing on the floor. It lacks class.

I suppose I should explain about our family, although that will be kind of hard, because all in all, they're pretty odd. There's the humans, of course. It's necessary to have at least one, because without opposable thumbs, I find it hard to run the can opener. Mr. and Mrs. Robertson are pretty nice as humans go. He's a software designer for computers, and has an office here in the house, so he's always home. Which is a bonus, because he seldom pays attention to anything except what he's working on. If I time it just right, he'll feed me again when he comes out to the kitchen for coffee, because he forgot he fed me when he got his last cup.

Mrs. Robertson is really great, but has something Mr. Robertson calls an "iron fist in a velvet glove". I'm not sure what that means, but I think she was a cat in another life. She can sure wrap him around her paw. I mean fingers. Even the kids will do what she tells them to. Although that might be a little different. She smiles sweetly at him, and stares at them with what they call "the look". I have tried that "look" on the can opener. It still won't run by itself. But it sure gets the kids moving pretty fast. If it weren't for her job at the police station, the kitchen would never be unmanned long enough for the kids to get into the cookie jar, and pass out the goodies.

Rebecca is cool, now. She's gotten past the stage of trying to paint my claws with fingernail polish, or braid beads into my tail. Hey! I got long hair, but not *that* long. They all call her Becca, even though she says that's not dignified at fifteen. Dignified? Obviously, she's never seen herself talking on the phone, folded sideways in the chair, winding her hair around her paw. I mean hand. She got braces this year. That was kind of a bummer, because for a long time she didn't smile like she used to. But she's still good for a cuddle, a chin scratch, and letting me sleep in her bed. She has my loyalty. And some of my hair on her clothes.

Stevie is a neat kid. He still likes Lego, and so do I. Can you imagine? Ten years old and already he wants to be an architect. When he's working on something, he gives me a block, and to please him, I bat it around for a while. Then when he leaves the bucket of Lego out, I can get down to some serious work. I never did get credit for that reproduction of the Eiffel Tower. He thought Becca did it as a joke.

Then there is...the dog. He's a Bassett Hound. If you've never seen one, think of a really big sausage that sags in the middle, and has four little stubby legs under it. Then stick on a big head with long ears. 'Walla', as the French say. You got a Bassett Hound. This one just missed the cut for being a show dog, and it's pretty clear, why. His ears are about six feet longer than they should be. Okay, it's an exaggeration, but he trips over them constantly...I mean the dog falls on his face so much, it's a wonder he doesn't have a Boxer nose. Now that would be cute. It's bad enough that he looks like someone cut him off at the knees. Oh yeah, his name is WattsOn. Yes, I know. Don't blame us animals for the names we get. Mr. Robertson loves old movies. He stays up sometimes and watches the black and white ones on the Late Show. Or he puts a tape in the VCR. We like them because it means he's on the couch with a bowl of popcorn, and other assorted snacks. If it's a really good movie, he forgets that he's feeding us instead of himself. Anyway, that's how the dog got his name. WattsOn was a present for Mr. Robertson's birthday. The kids gave him an Abbott and Costello videotape of their baseball skit. It's a routine where one human asks the other who's playing ball, and they say "Watts on second." All the humans think it's hilarious. They watch it and laugh, and the dog wags his tail. Says a lot for his IQ, doesn't it? WattsOn got changed to plain old Watson the next year when I came along.

My name is Holmes...Purrlock Holmes. I was Mr. Robertson's revenge, or so he said. I'm a cat, in case you haven't guessed. I was Mrs. Robertson's birthday present. The kids gave her some food bowls, a litter box, a scoop, and some kitty chow. I don't think she ever used any of them herself, but they did come in handy. Mr. R. picked out the cutest, cuddliest kitten in the litter. That would be me. He was all sloppy over the dumb dog. So now he snorts and mutters when Mrs. R. and I have schmooze time. Not where she can hear him, though. I butt her face and give her nose kisses, and I get anything I want. It's a talent, what can I say? Never works for dogs, because the appeal of those big brown eyes just doesn't outweigh the nausea caused by a blast of bone breath.

I'm a Birman. That means a long time ago, my great-great-great-great something or other, came from the country of Burma. Which is now called Myanmar. Humans never leave anything alone, not even names. My ancestors were noble cats that guarded sacred temples. I have a beautiful long coat that I groom constantly, because you never know when someone is going to be casting a cat food commercial. They might be looking for a handsome, regal animal with light hair, a dark mask, leggings, tail, ears, and the same sapphire blue eyes of the sacred goddess...and I have to be ready. Heaven forbid the white "gloves" on my feet should have a smudge on them.

I came with a big long pedigree and a fancy name. We don't talk about my name. Or put it this way--if the dog talks about it, his nose will not only be out of joint, but scratched by yours truly. It's his fault, I'm called Purrlock Holmes. Because he was Watson, Mrs. R. thought we should have a Sherlock. Then because I purred, it became Purrlock. You get the idea. If they'd only known then, that I would take up my namesake's profession, they might have preferred calling me "Couch Potato". It made no difference to me, anyway. I don't answer to anything except the call of nature, and the siren song of roast chicken in the oven.

I sniffed the air delicately, as I strolled into the kitchen, where the humans were all eating breakfast. Mmm...someone had bacon, but it was all gone. There is a difference between the odor of bacon that is available, and that which has been consumed by the inconsiderate and greedy. Sniff...sniff. Gross. Stevie hasn't changed those socks in a week. I gotta get out from under this table. Phew. Something died in those sneakers a month ago. Why can't the dog ever bury them instead of bones?

"Because that would be a bad thing. I'm not allowed to do bad things."

I might have known. There's the dog, laying beside Becca's chair. "Hey, get outta there. That's my territory."

"I didn't see your name written on the floor," Watson yawned in my face, and for a minute I thought I was downwind of some roadkill.

The choices were: smack him upside the head and listen to him yip (which is really satisfying at times), or take my dignity over to Mrs. R. who is always good for a soft touch. I flipped my tail up, turned and stalked to the other end of the table, sitting in my most regal pose, while ignoring lesser beings, in other words-- the dog.

"This is the fourth theft in two weeks, Edward. I just don't understand it." A small wedge of pancake appeared under the table in Mrs. R.'s hand. Ahh crispy and brown, just the way I liked it. I munched happily while the humans talked.

"Theft? What theft?" I couldn't see over the tabletop, but I could hear the rustle of the morning newspaper. Mr. R. was deep in the sports page. You can always tell how his teams are doing, by whether or not that section has the corners all twisted and ripped.

"Edward," Mrs. R. sighed. "You're not paying attention."

"Old man Mittlejohn's silver cigarette lighter." The somewhat milky reply managed to find its way out of the mouthful of cereal Stevie hadn't swallowed...or even chewed.

"Young *man*!" Ruh-roh. Even bets on whether he's in trouble for talking with his mouth full, or calling the elderly Mr. Mittlejohn "old man". I'd put my catnip on the last one. She's giving him "the look".

"The first one was Mrs. Perry's silver earrings. She left them on the patio table, and poof, they were gone." Becca added.

Mr. Robertson actually lowered the paper. I could see him now, because I'd jumped up onto the kitchen counter. The discussion must be getting serious, because nobody noticed I was headed for a bowl that still held a few last, luscious drops of pancake batter.

There's a knack to eating leftover pancake batter from a bowl, you know. Of course, I suppose humans don't have to worry about it, because you get all fussy and use a spoon. There's no challenge to that! Cats now, we make it an art. Fold whiskers back against the face, tilt ears to the rear at a forty-five degree angle, and stand as far from the bowl as you can, while still close enough to reach the good stuff. I worked my way down the inside, while tuning in to the details of the valuables that had been vanishing from our neighbor's houses.

"There was also a very old coin from Mr. Greenberg's collection. He called me about it, and I told him to report it to the station, but he thought they would just say he mislaid it. The same thing happened to Mrs. Thompson. She lost a sterling silver chain, just two days ago."

"Maybe there are aliens who are taking only silver things so they can fuel their space ship to return to the home planet!" Stevie cried.

"Maybe they'll kidnap some slaves, to keep it all polished," Becca leaned over the table and glared at him.

Stevie glared back. "Yeah? Well you better keep your mouth shut. Because there's enough metal in there to power them to- "

"Mommmmmmmmm!" Becca howled, stood up and stamped a foot at the same time.

Got to admire that girl. She could teach the dog a thing or two about coordination.

"School. Now." It was "the look" again. The kids left the table, Stevie with his eyes crossed when Mrs. R. was at the sink with their dishes, and Becca behind him, with her tongue stuck out. So much for dignity.

Me? I was sitting on the floor, performing my ritual "after pancake batter" face wash: two licks to the paw, one swipe over the left ear. Two licks to the paw, one swipe over the right ear. Personal hygiene is always important. Especially when you don't want to be caught with the batter on your whiskers.

"I hope they find out what's going on, soon." Mrs. R. frowned at the sink, which wasn't doing anything that I could see. "Really, Edward. People are feeling very nervous. These are all small things, but if they can be taken, so can larger things."

"Well dear, everything here is safe. I'm home most of the time, and we have Watson as a guard dog."

Oh gag me! I fell over on my side and lay there laughing, not that the humans could tell.

Mrs. Robertson patted him on the shoulder. "Edward, the house could be emptied of everything but your computer, and you'd never know it. Because Watson would be helping them carry it out."

"Would not!" came a woof from under the table.

"Would too!" I spit. Wait. We're starting to sound like the kids.

"See?" she gathered up her coat and car keys. "Even Purrlock agrees with me."

"But I'm sure the town's finest policemen will track down the thief in no time." Mr. R.'s eyes strayed longingly back to the paper and his sports scores.

"That's just the problem." With a snap, Mrs. R. shut her purse. "Nobody is reporting the thefts, because they are so small. But they're all talking about them, and now they're talking about it being someone in the neighbourhood. The one that gets mentioned the most, is Andrew. He and his father moved into the Hammond's old house just a couple of weeks ago. Andrew started doing chores for the neighbours right away. He's been in all the houses that have lost something. I also heard from Mrs. Shepherd that he's been in trouble already at school. And he's in Stevie's class, too. His parents divorced, and I think he's having a hard time of it. So he certainly doesn't need the other kids being cruel and taunting him about this, too." With a peck on Mr. R.'s cheek, she was gone for the day.

"It certainly is cruel." Mr. R. agreed, with a shake of the paper. "I can't believe that they sent Masterson down to the minors when that fat excuse for a pitcher couldn't strike out my grandmother on his best day."

Chapter Two

Making Tracks

"Got any plans for the day, Dumbo?" I walked over and poked the sausage…er, dog with my paw.

"Hey, cut that out," he whimpered. "I have very thin skin and your claws are sharp."

"I keep them sharp, in the event some nosey dog decides to inspect portions of my anatomy that are not public property." My eyes narrowed down to slits. I loved doing that. It always made Watson nervous. "Besides, your layer of blubber is so thick, I'd need a harpoon to get through it."

"Yeah? Well you have tuna breath."

I fluffed myself up to full size and watched the canine coward, back away. "I do *NOT!*" When he'd shivered long enough, I deflated my fur. "You know they won't feed me the real stuff."

"Okay," he sniffed. "But you were mean to say I'm fat."

"I didn't say you were fat, I said you had blubber." Let him figure that out. If he can. "Come on, time is wasting and we have work to do."

"Work?" Watson tripped over his ears, but managed to stay upright, as we headed for the doggie door.

"Work. We're going to make the rounds of the neighbourhood, and find out just what is going on here."

"But you're not allowed outside." He stopped and stared at me. What, did I sprout an extra tail or something?

"There is 'not allowed', and 'not known' about," I said patiently. "What the humans don't know, won't hurt them. And if you tell them, I will hurt you. Clear?"

"You are just so mean," Watson whimpered, as we scooted through his doggy door and out into the yard.

Chapter Three

The First Clues

Dogs come in handy, even if it's just to do things for you. Watson held up a board in the back yard fence, so I could wriggle through. Then I had to wait for him to huff, puff and dig his way underneath.

"Cut back on the kibble and you wouldn't have that problem," I sighed as we headed down the street for the Perry's house.

"What are we going to do?" I had to slow down so the dog could keep up and not waddle himself into exhaustion before we even got started. He trotted with his head back, so his ears only scraped the ground, instead of sweeping it. I often thought that if he had muscles *in* his ears, instead of between his ears, that he could just stick them out sideways, and in a good breeze it would be like hydroplaning.

Regretfully, I passed by the Keirstead's flowerbed, with its birdbath full of sparrows, and kept on going. Not that I would bother them, mind you. At least, not in any really serious way like...eating them. But I did occasionally get an urge to inspect the pattern of their feathers at close range.

"I think we need the inside scoop. First, we'll check with the Perry's Schnauzer. He's a pretty sharp cookie."

"He's outside in his kennel during the day. I'll bet he didn't see anything." I could hear Watson starting to pant. But at least with his head tipped back, his breath was going to peel the bark off the tree branches overhead instead of stripping my fur.

"No problem. We'll check anyway. Ahh...here's the back yard." I cruised in under a lilac bush and looked around to see where we could get in. "Oh great. Chain-link fencing. I can get over it, but what am I going to do with you?"

Watson started to whine, "But I want to go, too."

"Oh shut up, crybaby. Look, there's a latch. I can climb the fence, open the gate, and we're in. But let's make this quick, because I don't want anyone finding that gate open, and closing it again while we're inside."

"Aw, you care. You really care!" The curved piece of steel cable that Watson called a tail, started whipping around.

"Hey, watch it fella. Those are my whiskers. All I care about is not getting you 'grounded'. Somebody has to get me in and out of our own yard."

"Oh." I heard a sniff. Geez, now his feelings are hurt.

"You go over to the corner there and let him know we're here. If he starts barking, the game's up."

"Okay." Ears dragging, my sidekick trotted off. Then tripped and fell on his face. His first rumbling woof, was muffled by a mouth full of grass. A minute later, he looked back to the bush and nodded. I made a dash for the gate, was up the wire and undid the latch in record time. Then a few quick licks to the fur to make myself presentable, and we moseyed around the corner of the garage.

Pascal, the Perry's Schnauzer, was sitting inside his run. His humans had built him an extra long, fenced-in run with an insulated doghouse, and even windows that opened to catch a breeze. When they were home, he lived in the house like a normal dog.

There are Schnauzers, and there are *Schnauzers.* Pascal was one of the last kind. He was big. I mean biggggg. I weigh twelve pounds. Watson the Fat weighs 50 if he weighs an ounce. Pascal weighs three times that. At least we can sit in his shade, while we talk.

"So, how's it going Pasc?" I joined him in sitting, then looked up. I'm gonna get a crick in my neck if we're here too long. Watson flopped on the grass outside the run, and saved his neck by rolling over on his back. Trust him to look for clues while his eyes were closed.

"Can't complain," he woofed. "Get my two squares a day, lots of exercise, scratches when I ask for them, and a new bone every week."

"I had a bone," Watson moaned dreamily. "But I lost it."

"You buried it," I corrected.

"Oh. Do you know where?"

I sighed and thought about telling him it was probably in the same place where he lost his mind, but then I'd have to explain to him what a "mind" was.

Instead, I held my tongue and turned back to the Schnauzer. "We just dropped in to ask you about Mrs. Perry losing her earrings. I don't suppose you saw who took them, or it would be all over the neighbourhood by now. You know that Shih Tzu next door can't keep its trap shut."

"Hehe. That's true." Pascal lifted a massive hind foot and scratched his ear. "Too bad I didn't see anything. But I was in the house when it happened. You know what humans are like- Mrs. Perry was in a hurry because she was late for a meeting, after supper. I was lying by the door, when she went out to the patio to find Mr. Perry. I saw her trying to put the earrings on as she went. Funny creatures, humans." He paused, thoughtfully. "Put holes in their ears then stick something in them." Then he sat there, staring off into space. Far be it for me to be rude, especially to anything that big, but we weren't going to get anywhere, if we waited for him to figure out humans.

"So how did they disappear?"

"Well," Pascal pawed his nose and thought some more. "The kids called me just then, but I saw her put them down on the patio table. She came back inside, to tell the kids to take me to the park, and when she went back out, we could all hear her asking who had taken her earrings. But we were in the living room except for Mr. Perry. And it turns out he was next door borrowing the Sawyer's garden hose."

"Did you look for them? I mean like really close to the ground?" Trust Watson to pipe up with a prize thought like that. Who could get closer to it than him?

"Yeah, we all did. Although they put me back in my run. Said I might step on one and get it in my foot." Pascal shrugged and laid down. Ahhhhhhh…relief. I could bend my neck again.

"Hmm. Not much to go on, but we'll keep making the rounds." I gave the big boy a high five, and motioned to Watson to get a move on. "Wait a minute." I stopped and turned back. "What colour were the earrings?"

"Silver. Just plain old silver. Big hoops they were."

As we made our way back across the lawn and around the trees in the Perry's yard, I pondered the mystery of the missing earrings. They couldn't have been outside on that table very long. And someone would have had to open the gate or climb the fence, cross the yard, and get onto the patio to reach them. Then be off before they were caught. I mean, those earrings didn't just fly off by themselves did they?

I was just working out the calculation of how much time it would take a human to do all that, when my sidekick wandered off course with a gleam in his eye, and a twitch in his hind leg. He was eyeing a big maple tree.

"C'mon," I hauled him back towards the fence by one of his four thousand rolls of loose skin. "Over-watering of trees can be very harmful."

Chapter Four

Something Fishy

"What now?" The dog stood guard while I pawed the Perry's gate shut, then we were on our way over to the next street and Mr. Mittlejohn's house. As we slipped out of the yard, something moved deeper into the lilac bushes. There was no time for idle curiosity, or I'd have sent the pooch to check it out. It was always good to keep an eye on who was wandering around your neighborhood, especially when things were disappearing.

"Now we find out what happened to the lighter." I stepped carefully between the rows of peas in the Browns' garden, while Watson thundered down the narrow strip of grass that led to the path next door. His speed was almost enough to ruffle the leaves of the flowers planted in neat rows on each side of the path.

This was going to be more of a challenge. Mr. Mittlejohn lived by himself. He might know Watson, but I was going to stick out like a sore thumb. People on our street were pretty responsible, and cats didn't just roam outside. Besides, as a highly pedigreed, extremely handsome example of my breed, I was never allowed out of the house, except in our yard.

We circled the house, wondering how to reach our informant. I briefly considered trying the doorknob, because standing on my hind legs, I could reach it with my front paws. But then I thought about Mrs. Orkenhaller, who lived next door. She was an older lady who didn't get out much, so she liked to sit at the window and watch what went on around the neighborhood. The trouble was, she couldn't see really well, and sometimes called the police about really weird stuff. Like the time she reported Mr. Knutson for burying a body in his backyard when he was digging a trench to lay his rose tree in for the winter. I guess the tree all wrapped up in burlap looked kind of like a human...all lumpy and that. So you can imagine what would happen if she saw me trying to open a door. "Hello, Police Department? There's a three-foot bear wearing a mask, breaking into the house next door. Come quick!" Nope. Couldn't take the risk, although it might be pretty funny. So we kept trekking around the outside of the house.

Then, bingo...I saw it. An open window in the study. Right in front of the goldfish tank. And a tree beside the window. Up I went.

"That's not fair," Watson woofed.

"Shhhhhhh you numbskull. You want to get us busted?" I hissed down at him. My ancestral genes kicked in, and I slunk along the branch like the greatest of jungle cats. Although when I slipped right before jumping to the window ledge, it took some of the polish off my performance. I stepped delicately over the sill and pressed my nose to the glass of the tank. A large goldfish, with elegant, white and orange fins, drifted over to me.

"You hadn't better be thinking of lunch," Watson sniffed.

"Quiet, peasant. I am communing." And I was. The vibrations were coming through the water to my nose. "Hey Goldie. Got anything for us on the missing lighter?"

And if I did, what could you do about it? You're a cat.

"Yes, but I have a dog with me."

Oh great. A cat working with a dog. What next?

'Lunch' I thought to myself. But no...this was more important. "Maybe a fish fry, hmmmmmm? Come on. We want to find out who's taking stuff in the neighbourhood. Everybody is talking about the new kid, Andrew. Be kind of a shame to see him take the rap if he didn't do it."

Oh yeah. I know him. He cleans my tank for Mr. Mittlejohn. Does a real nice job, too. Even scrubbed off my castle, and washed the gravel.

"Is it true he does chores for the other neighbors, too?"

Sure. Goldie's fins wafted back and forth in the water. They were so...attractive. *He helped Mr. Perry unload the cement blocks for that barbecue pit he's building. Then the Schneider's parrot told me he gets paid to catch crickets for Mr. Greenberg's turtle.*

"Wait a minute. The parrot told you? How did he manage that from six houses down the street?" My tail was lashing. I just couldn't help myself.

"Hurry up," yipped the overgrown puppy on the ground. "I think I hear the mailman."

Goldie rolled her eyes. Which was quite a trick for a fish. *The parrot told the Roger's ferret. The ferret told the Munson's potbelly pig, and the pig squealed to the Arden's rabbit, next door. He likes to nibble the dandelions under the tree you almost fell out of.*

"I did not almost fall out," I huffed. "I was testing the flexibility of the branch."

"Did too." Oh great. Now Dumbo is barking up the right tree at the wrong time.

"Shut up down there, I can't hear the fish flapping its lips." I pressed my nose flatter against the tank. Much more of this, and I'd be cross-eyed like that Siamese of the Turners.

"And the other neighbours? What other houses does Andrew go to?"

*Let me see...*Goldie opened and closed her mouth a few times. *There's Thompsons. I know he mows their grass. He does yard work for the Andersons and Townsends too.*

"Okay, that gives us a list to work on. Now tell me about the lighter. How did it disappear?"

Goldie flapped a gill. That's as close to shrugging as a goldfish can get, since they don't have shoulders.

I have no idea. It was a really nice afternoon, and Mr. Mittlejohn left the window open like it is now. Just about anything could get in there. She turned sideways, so one eye glared at me.

I had the feeling I was being singled out. *And he went over to the Rogers' house to drive Mrs. Rogers to the doctor. She's about to spawn again. I don't think he locked the door, either. Last I saw of it, the lighter was on the desk, because the sun was shining on it, and I had a hard time getting to sleep, the way the sun glared off the silver.*

For a brief moment, I had a vision of the nice human Mrs. Rogers with a baby carriage full of little fish. "Great. Thanks, kid. We'll let you know if we find out anything." I shinnied down the tree in double quick time. "Come on, Watson. Next stop, the Greenbergs."

As we trotted down the driveway, a shadow moved away from the hedge next door. Either I was hallucinating from hunger (I hadn't eaten in an hour), or my mind was still on the way those fins lifted, and floated...so delicate...so delightful...so delicious...

Chapter Five

Snap It Up!

This was going to be a cinch. The Greenbergs have a screened in porch. The outside door is never locked, although the door into the house is. A claw just inside the frame and that baby opens like a dream. We'll have to be careful though. I don't think they've oiled the hinges lately. If I have to open it any wider for the Snausage Snapper here, we could be in trouble. It's a good thing the Greenbergs are both at work.

"Wow, this is cool." Watson stood just inside the porch, head wagging back and forth so fast, his ears qualified as dangerous weapons. You'd think he'd never seen a sun porch full of wicker furniture and more green ferns than a rain forest.

"Yeah, yeah. Just don't shed on anything. We don't want to leave a trail behind." I jumped onto a bookcase, and surveyed the length of the porch. Our informant had to be here, somewhere.

"Me shed? Look who's talking! Becca says there is enough hair on her clothes to make another cat out of. Sometimes I wish she would make another cat. One that is nicer. And doesn't shed."

Whine, whine, whine, that's all the dog ever does.

"Get this- there *is* no other cat. There is only me. There will only ever *be* me. I am your worst nightmare, so don't fall asleep tonight. And keep the noise down. I have to talk to someone." I leapt from the top of the bookcase, down to a table, and pushed my way through a row of potted plants. A feathery leaf ran under my nose and I sneezed.

"Bless you," Watson mumbled, grudgingly.

"Thank you." My life is complete. I have been blessed by a dog. Geesh. Aha...there he is.

I laid down alongside a tank that sat on a lower table, almost hidden by a potted palm tree. There was a pump, quietly circulating water, and a lamp over top, shining light on an empty shell. Well, it looked empty. The shell was sitting on a rock shelf in the tank, and it looked like there was nobody home.

"Hello? Hello?" I tapped politely on the back of the shell with one claw.

Four legs shot out around the edges of the shell, and a big, ugly head poked its way out the front. The turtle stretched his neck, looked me up and down and blinked. "Yeah, whaddya want?"

"Hi, Calvin, I'm Purrlock Holmes, from down the street. You don't know me, but-- "

"Don't know you? Hah. The whole neighbourhood knows you. The crystal vase, caper? The night you fell in the pool when you slipped outside, then stuck your ugly mug against the window and scared the life out of the Robertson's company? And let us not forget the hamster. Wasn't it you that taught poor Hamlet how to play 'Hide 'N Eat'?"

If there's one thing I hate, it's a know-it-all that knows nothing. "The vase was the dog's fault."

"Was *not*!" How does a dog manage to sound indignant while yipping?

"He chased me through the house, and I jumped to the mantel in self-defence. The vase only got broke, because when I jumped from there to the dining room table and into the mashed potatoes, the bowl skidded and I couldn't get my claws into anything to avoid the flowers. So there."

"Yeah, right." Calvin dipped his head under the water and brought it back out. "Is that hamster fur on your whiskers?"

"I did not eat that hamster!" Cool. I have to be Mr. Cool, here. The turtle cannot get to me. I am a noble cat. The descendant of a long line of sacred cats. We do not let smart aleck turtles annoy us. And besides, when I growled, it made Watson nervous. All I can see now, is his butt sticking out from under the couch. "I did not eat the hamster," I repeated calmly, "that was the Totten's tabby. You remember him--the one that the kids dressed up as a baby doll for Hallowe'en. He was never the same, after. And he didn't eat it. He just...held it hostage for a bit, er, I mean a while."

Calvin was blowing bubbles in the water. Why did I have the feeling this was the turtle equivalent of a "raspberry"?

"Listen Cal, we don't have a lot of time here, but we'd like to know what happened to that coin of Mr. Greenberg's. We're cruising the neighbourhood to check out all these things that have gone missing. If someone doesn't find the real culprit, that new little boy down the street is going to get blamed for it."

The big green head swivelled towards me and stared. "Worms," he said, then drew himself back into his shell.

Was he implying that *I*, the most fastidious, and cleanest of animals had--

"One will do. About two inches. I like them on the lean side, and don't forget to clean the dirt off." His voice echoed from inside the shell. "You want information, you're gonna pay for it."

Oh great. We were being held up by a turtle. I jumped down off the table and tapped Watson on the back. He jumped so high he hit his head on the underside of the couch, and crawled out howling.

"You scared me," he cried.

"You scared yourself in the hall mirror, last night." I sighed. "Listen, he's holding the information ransom for a--a worm. Can you go dig one up?"

"Digging is a bad thing, and I'm not allowed to do bad things," he chanted. There were times that Enormous Ears got on my nerves. This was one of them.

I grabbed him each side of his silly drooping face with my paws (claws in), and snarled "We need a worm. Get one. Now."

"Okay, okay. Don't get your tail kinked." He wiggled out of my grip. "You have to open the door for me when I get back. You *will* open it, won't you?" Watson glared.

"I have to. I need a worm." What I didn't say, was that I'd have to let two in, to get the one that I wanted.

"And not in the flower garden," I hollered as he trotted down the steps and started to quarter the lawn. I was letting him back in, not two minutes later.

"Hey, that was quick."

"Mmpf." He dropped the pink-brown squiggling thing on the floor. "Yeah. A robin dropped it. I promised to leave him some turned up in the dirt behind our garage, later."

Now how was I supposed to get the stupid thing up to the turtle tank. Not…not in my *mouth*! Gross. Just too gross.

"Look," I stared at the worm. "This is your destiny. The turtle wants a worm. We got him a worm. If I pick you up and you so much as think about crossing my lips, I will turn you into worm burger." With my lips curled back as far as they could go, I picked up the worm in my teeth. I jumped onto the bookcase, over to the table and was dropping that sucker into the tank before Watson's butt touched the floor. I politely turned my head to the window as Calvin chowed down.

"Okay," he burped. "What did you want to know?"

"What was stolen, and who took it?"

"Can't tell you all that," he blinked in the sun and smacked his lips again. Over a worm. Egad. "All I can tell you, is that Mr. Greenberg uses that desk over there, to lay out his coin collection, and last Wednesday, he was checking a magazine for some of the ones he wants, and he had laid out one set. Then the phone rang. When he came back, one of the coins was gone. I wouldn't have known about it at the time, but I heard him telling Mr. Perry."

"Hmm." I rubbed a paw up over my ear.

"You got fleas? 'Cause I hear cats carry fleas a lot." Calvin narrowed his eyes. He was either getting nasty, or sleepy. It was hard to tell.

"No! I don't have fleas or worm--oh, never mind." This wasn't getting us anywhere. Better get the rest of the scoop and visit the last victims. "What was taken?"

"A silver dollar," Calvin yawned. "It was valuable, I guess."

Things were starting to look brighter…almost as shiny as silver. "How did the thief get in?"

"Got me," Calvin splayed his legs out under the lamp and stretched his neck. "Ahhh love that heat. Good thing it was warm like this when that raccoon ripped the screen."

My razor sharp senses pounced on his last remark. "You mean that screen was open? The same day the coin was stolen?"

The big green head was drooping slowly, eyes closing as it went. "Yup. Mr. Greenberg took it out in the morning. Had to wait all day for the carpenter to come and put a new one in. That's okay though. I caught two flies and a spider. They were yummy." Calvin smiled as he drifted off to sleep.

"I'm beginning to see a pattern," I announced to Watson.

He looked down at the carpet. "I don't see a pattern, just speckles of black in the green."

I slapped a paw to my forehead. Why me? Why was I gifted with God's joke on the world? "A pattern to the crimes, Sherlock. Now come on. We got to hit the Thompsons' place before their kids get home from school."

"But you're Sherlock. I mean Purrlock. I'm Watson." The dog was born confused, and appears to be incurable. I opened the door for us both, and we slipped from the front yard, to the forsythia at the side of the yard.

"Did you see that?" I grabbed him by an ear and pointed towards the empty garbage can. They had been collected that morning, so no self-respecting cat or dog would be bothered with them till at least tomorrow.

"What? What?" he yelped.

"I saw something. Something at the Perry's and Mr. Mittlejohn's too." I crouched and let my eyes turn into slits. We were being followed. I was sure of it.

Chapter Six

The Ditzy Furball

My feet dragged a little as we trotted along the row of dwarf cedar trees that line the Thompsons' driveway. The dog even got ahead of me.

"Will you hurry up?" he nagged. "Or do I have to run a can opener to get you moving faster?"

I briefly considered a little something from the medicine cabinet to make him "run" faster, but I'm not that mean. Really. I just wasn't looking forward to our next interview.

"Now what?" Watson plunked his fat butt on the grass beside the back door and waited for me to make the next move. I supposed I had to do it. As little as I was looking forward to this, I walked him around the corner to the other end of the house, secluded by trees. Extending from the Thompson's bedroom window, was a wire enclosure with shelves, a velvet pillow, scratching post, awning, in short--everything a fat, pampered, egotistical, snotty Persian needed. And there she was…Brunhilde.

I hopped up on a little patio table, the better to see her magnificence. I might as well say it, because she'd tell you that's why I wanted to get closer to her, anyway. Watson managed to clamber up onto a deck chair.

"Hiya Hildy," I smiled sweetly. Oh, this was going to be hard. But there are small ways of making it easier. Like using her detested nickname.

"That's Brunhilde, to you, Fat Boy. And don't you forget it."

I looked at her magnificence overflowing the pillow, and thought about human sayings like 'that's the pot calling the kettle, black'. She had thick, white fur. Miles and miles of it. If Becca could make another cat out of what I shed, they could make a pride of lions out of what Beefy Brunhilde left behind her. Her eyes were green, and looked tiny in that squished up face with the piggy nose.

"Look but don't touch," she purred throatily. Oh great. Now she thought I was there for pleasure…hers.

"Um, Hil…Brunhilde, we're trying to get a handle on who has been taking things around the neighbourhood. We thought maybe those gorgeous, emerald green eyes of yours might have seen something the humans didn't, when Mrs. Thompson's chain disappeared." I choked a little on the flattery, but hey…whatever it takes to get Miss Piggy talking.

"Well, can't say as I did," she stretched along the shelf, fat and fur overflowing the edge. "They had opened the window for me to come out and greet my many admirers, while they got dressed to go out for dinner. She was wearing a deep purple satin dress. V-neck, not too short. The colour is all wrong with my eyes, but she never listens."

My tail was starting to twitch. I'm an impatient kind of guy. "What about this silver chain?"

"Oh that." A sigh followed, as if it was an effort for her to think. And for her, it probably was. "Mrs. Thompson put me up on my pillow…did you notice how it matches my eyes?…and she had this chain and pendant in her hand. Then as she was smoothing down my beautiful fur, she dropped it through the wire and it fell on the ground."

"So you saw who took it, right?" I leaned forward, even though it brought me closer to the Persian porker. "It wasn't Andrew, was it?"

"Who? Oh him. The grass cutter. I never even saw him that day. And my kingdom does need to be clipped, ever so delicately. We can't ruin that delightful green grass that matches my eyes...did you notice how they match?" She batted her eyelashes to make sure I noticed.

"Yes, I did. They're lovely." Okay, so I lie on occasion. Sue me. "But how did the chain disappear then?"

"Well, don't ask *me*!" she sniffed. "All I know, is that when Mrs. Thompson went outside to get it, all that was left in the grass, was the pendant. It was lavender jade."

"But that doesn't make sense," I told her. "Why would anyone steal a silver chain and leave a valuable pendant behind?"

"Do I *look* like Miss Marple? She's old and wrinkled. I saw her on the PBS movie. I, on the other hand, am young and beeeyootiful." Brunhilde rolled over on her back and extended her paws above her to admire the polish on her claws. I bet Becca taught Sally Thompson how to do that.

"Yeah, well...we got to be on our way. Time and crime wait for no man...or dog and cat."

"Mmmm yes," she purred, rolling over to face me, eyes narrowed to little green slits. "You're out without permission, aren't you?" Her tail flipped, lashed out, and flipped again. She was thinking. That meant trouble for everyone.

"I have a note from my vet that I need more fresh air." I lie. But I didn't say I was good at it.

"Mr. Thompson's cell phone is on the dresser. The Robertson's number is keyed on pad number eight. One push, and I could tell your humans where you are." No doubt about it. She had a nasty smile. If that's what it was.

"You...ah, you don't really want to do that, do you?" I could never get home before the phone rang, even if I ran and left the bumbling Basset Hound behind.

"Oh but I do, I do." Now she was upright, tail still swishing. My, what big eyes you have Brunhilde. I decided to call her bluff.

"And what are you going to do? Meow at Mr. Robertson?" I laughed heartily, expecting Watson to join in. His only contribution was a snore. He'd fallen asleep.

"Of course not, you idiot. The Schneiders are on speed dial too. I'll call their parrot, and he'll spill the beans for me. Your human will never know it's not Mr. Schneider. I may even have him embroider the tale a little. Perhaps something about…a hamster."

"I did not eat that darned hamster! Nobody ate that hamster! I have never had a hamster in my mouth!" I was so mad I jumped at the wire of her sun porch, and clung there. She never blinked an eye.

"You're so…cute, with your face squished against that wire, Big Guy. Believe me, it's an improvement." She examined a paw, licked it, and patted a hair back into place. "Tell you what." Suddenly she was all business. "Next time the Robertsons have a party and you snag a whole wedge of Cheddar, it gets delivered here. Immediately."

"How did you know about that?" I was so startled, I almost let go of the wire.

"I have my sources." Brunhilde got up, hoisted her tail to full mast, and strolled back inside the house.

I let go of the wire, and dropped to the ground, slapping a paw at the deck chair where Watson was still snoring. If I hadn't been so rattled, I'd have hit him instead of the chair. It folded up, with Watson inside. By the time I pried him out, we were pushing the deadline for getting home ahead of the kids. How did I know? Because animals have extra senses. And I could see the clock inside the Thompson's bedroom.

"Don't run!" Watson howled, as he galloped through the hedge back to our own street. But I had a plan. Unfortunately, when I stopped to put it into action, Watson ran into me from behind and we both fell into the ditch.

"Quick!" I smacked him with a paw and pointed to the Spruce tree at the end of the Green's driveway. "There he goes. Sick 'em, boy!"

"Where? Where? Who? Who?" Watson clambered back out of the ditch. His head snapped back and forth, as his ears slapped me across the face.

"There!" I grabbed his head in both front paws to stop the torture, and then pointed. "Under that tree. I saw something move. Maybe a leg or a tail. Someone has been following us all day. Now go get him!"

Watson took off at a lumbering run. Given his speed, I figured someone could cut the tree down, saw it up, build a couple of picnic tables and have the picnic, before he got there. But he was earnest, if not fast. His nose was to the ground, and he was searching.

"No luck," he sighed, trotting back to where I was hiding behind some rose bushes. "The Turner's Pug has been here. He hasn't had his nails clipped yet. You can see the marks they leave. Van Wort's Samoyed is shedding. I smelled a couple of strange cats, and a new dog. Saw some human sneaker prints. The Reed's puppy is still chewing shoes, I can tell. Oh yeah...and Fifi, the poodle from the next street has a new rhinestone collar."

Just for a second, I forgot about our mystery. I could understand his nose work... I could even understand him recognizing the print of chewed shoes...but the collar? "How can you tell, by looking under the tree, that Fifi has a new collar?"

Watson looked at me like I had fallen off the kibble caboose and landed on my head. "I can't. I saw her in the next yard, talking to that flashy Doberman."

Dogs. You can't live with them, and you can't live without them. Although there are times like this, that I'd like to try.

Chapter Seven

A Little Something

Watson pushed the bottom of the board in the fence, and I slithered through into our own yard. I even held a corner while he shoved, grunted, pushed, and hauled his carcass through the opening. Why couldn't he have been a guinea pig or something? At least they're intelligent, and there's already a small hole over in the corner, that the chipmunks use to run in and out. Oh yeah. I forgot. I need him to open the fence for me.

I sat down on the lawn and carefully groomed all traces of our secret expedition out of my fur. Watson shook himself, got dirt on me, and I had to start all over. But that was okay. We were about to catch our "shadow".

Very casually I started strolling across the lawn, cutting a path just behind the garage. I turned my head as if to speak to the pooch behind me, then with lightning fast reflexes, I pounced towards the garage wall.

"Got you!" I wasn't quite sure what I had, though. It was small, furry and wiggling.

"Let me go, please! Don't hurt me. I'm sorry, please let me go, I won't come back again."

Cautiously I lifted my paw. Now granted, my paws are big, but this was just a little scrap of fur. I couldn't even tell what kind of fur, till the head came up, and two big yellow and green eyes looked at me. Good grief. It was a kitten. The slinking, sneaking, shadow that was tracking our every move, was nothing more than a baby. He cowered back against the wall, and shivered so hard, I had serious concerns about Mr. Robertson's tools falling off their hooks, inside.

"Why were you following us?" I leaned over him. A little intimidation never hurts.

"I- I was trying to find a way home," he sniffed. "I thought if I followed you, you might know where I lived."

With a sigh, I sat back. I had a fleeting idea that whoever was following us, might be the thief. But it looked like one of Mrs. Perry's earrings would make a good collar for this guy, he was that small. "Okay, well let's start with who are you and where do you live? Because you see, we know all the animals in this neighbourhood, and they're …uh…well…you know…they don't have any babies."

"I don't know," he whispered, head drooping. "W--I never had a name. And I don't know where I was born. There were some humans. And they were very loud and angry. Then one day, a big truck came, and all the things from the house were taken out, and the humans got in their car. Nobody came back for u--me."

Kid was stumbling a lot. Looked scared. Looked hungry, too. I laid down on the grass and hoped none of it would stain the white on my feet. I couldn't make myself any smaller, so this would have to do.

"How did you get here?" I asked him.

The grey and black stripes shook a little more. If he kept this up, I was going to get seasick, watching him. "I kept looking for my people. Sometimes I went to a door and they chased me away with a broom. Or there were dogs...big dogs!" He crouched down again, and almost vanished into the blades of grass. "They chased me. Their people threw rocks at me."

Just to make sure nobody could see how bad I felt, I licked my side, and nibbled on a claw. "So you can't find your home, and you've had nothing to eat?"

"No, sir."

I coughed. Hair in my throat. Don't think for one minute, I was getting soft. "Well, what do you normally eat?" It had been a while since I was a kitten. All I could really remember was warm fur, and Mom.

"Well...I had a Mom once, but she went away. Then my humans went away." The little head drooped, but not before I could see the big eyes filling up. Aw for cripes sake. He was crying.

"You made him cry!" Watson would choose that moment to add to my personal guilt trip.

"A dog! It's a dog! Help, oh help please! He'll eat me, he'll kill me, he'll pull out my fur and my whiskers--"

"Slow down, Sonny." I put a paw, very gently, on top of the quivering kitten. "This is Watson. As dogs go, he's pretty good. He doesn't chase cats. We hashed that out when I first came to live here. And as long as you stay upwind of his breath, he's okay to live with."

Watson laid down on the grass and tried to flatten himself. He even whimpered in sympathy. Geez, all we needed was music from one of those sappy human movies.

"But he's a dog!" the kid insisted. "He'll bark. Then people will come and find me, and they'll take me to that place that cats don't come back from." Poor guy. He was so frantic now his little legs were going like a windmill and he caught me a good one across the nose. Oh so faintly, I heard a snicker from behind me.

"I wouldn't do that," Watson rumbled. "Really, I wouldn't. I like cats." Wow. That must have cost him something to say. I was truly impressed, until he added "Some cats."

"What are you going to do with me?" the furball asked.

Now that he was a little calmer, I took my paw away, and rubbed it alongside my face. "Good question. We can't sneak you into the house. It's kind of hard to go trotting past humans with a kitten in your mouth."

"If you could distract them, I could sneak him in, and hide him in Stevie's room. Mrs. R. says she can never find anything in there." Watson had big ears, a big mouth, and a big heart. Sometimes it was very hard to dislike him. I would have to work harder on forgiving him for being a dog.

"Maybe." I thought for a minute. "Look, I have to get inside now, before someone comes home and finds me out here. Let's go in, and we'll figure out what to do, from there."

"That's okay. I don't mind being alone." The furball sniffed. One more tug at the heartstrings and I was going to be a basket case.

"Look, we'll be back. I promise. Come on, we'll find you a place to hide till then." With a nudge of my nose, I got him up and wobbling across the lawn. When you saw the whole kitten, what there was of something that small, he was kind of cute. The striped suit was nifty, and came with white gloves and a white shirt-front. We shepherded him across the lawn and under the edge of the patio.

"Now look, Kid." Geez, we can't keep calling him that. Wait…yes, we can. He doesn't have another name, and it will do for now. "I'm going to call you Kid. If that's okay with you."

He seemed to perk up a little. "Is that my name now? I never had a name before."

"Yeah, that's your name. I'm Purrlock, and the dog there is Watson," I nodded to the dog, who for once, had kept his distance and was waiting quietly by the back steps. "You stay here, okay? I mean right here. No wandering off. I can't always get out you know, and I don't want to send the dog off alone to look for you. He gets lost in the back yard."

"I promise." The kid crawled under a giant dandelion someone had missed with the weed snipper, and crouched down.

"We'll be back." I patted his head, and nodded mine towards the back door. Watson got up and opened the doggy door for me.

As luck would have it, the kids came in the front door, as we slipped through the back one. After a frenzy of barking (Watson), baby talk (Becca) and rubs and scratches (Stevie), we followed them upstairs.

"I got a friend coming over," Stevie's yell was muffled by the shirt he was pulling over his head. He flung it onto the pile on his bedroom floor. "Don't hog the phone, eh?"

"Friends are for after homework, remember?" Becca called from down the hallway. She had already carefully folded her school clothes and laid them in the laundry hamper. Now dressed in jeans and a sweatshirt, she laid out books and pens on her desk. Amazing. Her bed looks like a bomb hit it, but there isn't a paper or pantyhose out of place anywhere else in the room.

"Nyah hah!" Her brother yanked his door open, and stuck his head out "*I* don't have any. So there."

Becca took this inequality very well. She opened her own door, yelled "Go soak your head!" then slammed it shut again.

Downstairs, the phone was ringing. Stevie galloped down to answer it, and we snuck into Mr. and Mrs. R's bedroom. Not that we had to, but it was always so neat and clean that we were afraid of leaving a dirty paw print. Then we'd be shut out, and lose the chance to sit on their window seat that looked out on the backyard. I had to push a footstool over so Watson could get up. It was a nice view out over the lawn and into other yards. But right now, my mind was on something else.

"He's awfully small to be out there alone," Watson sighed.

"I know." There was nothing moving around the patio, that

I could see. Let's hope it stayed that way.

"But I'll protect him," he woofed sternly. "Nobody is going to chase him when I'm around."

I looked at the dog. Any other time I'd have fallen off my seat, laughing. He would choose now, to be so...nice.

"We can't work on the Kid problem, till the humans are out of the way. Let's see what we've got on the robberies. Now, what were Mrs. Perry's earrings?"

"Silver."

"And the lighter?"

"Silver."

"The coin of Mr. Greenberg's?"

"Silver." Watson was starting to get excited, nodding as he answered. I backed another foot away from his ears.

"Then Mrs. Thompson's chain?"

"Silver!" he yelped.

"Which means they all have what, in common?"

Watson's brow wrinkled. At least now, it matched the rest of him. "They were stolen?" he asked hopefully.

I banged my head against the window. It didn't help, but then again, it couldn't hurt. Ouch. I was wrong.

"No, dummy. They were all silver. Who would want silver things? And why did they leave the pendant, and only take the silver chain?"

A massive rumble broke the silence. "Sorry," Watson blushed, as much as possible for a Basset. "It's close to supper, and thinking makes me hungry."

"Breathing makes you hungry." I muttered. No, that was an uncharitable thought. I really would have to stop that. Some day. But for now, the answer to our mystery was close…I could sense it…almost smell it. Or was that dinner, cooking?

"Is there something wrong?" the dog stared as I paced back and forth on the seat. "Do you have worms?"

"*NO*! I do *NOT* have worms. And I did not eat the hamster!" I screamed.

"Purrlock…." The warning drifted up from downstairs. I really had to learn to control myself. I jumped down and stalked out of the room, followed by the mutt.

"But I didn't say anything about a hamster," he puzzled. "Do they give you worms?"

Chapter Eight

It Tasted Like Chicken

I was right. Supper was cooking. I floated into the kitchen on a cloud of chicken smells. And there it was, right on the counter. A big platter of chicken pieces, all golden, and juicy, and just waiting.

"You're drooling," Watson yipped.

"Am not. Dogs drool. Cats rule."

I was almost hypnotized by the aroma when it struck me-- chicken minus human, equals available food. It's very simple math. Work it out for yourself.

"Run under Mrs. R's feet and yelp your head off," I snapped at the dog. For once, he did what he was told. Watson trotted off towards the cupboard then rolled over on the floor yelping and howling, and generally trying very hard to make it an Oscar winning performance. He failed miserably, but it served my purpose. Mrs. R. bent over him, Becca put down the dishes and bent over him, and I leapt for the cupboard. I grabbed the nearest chicken leg and streaked for the door to the hallway, taking the corner to upstairs so fast the hall rug slid over and knocked down the umbrella stand. Even over the crash of metal on a tile floor, and the rumble of assorted baseballs and other junk pouring out of the stand, I could still hear something annoying. Right behind me was the Wounded Wonder, barking "Share! Share! Share!"

As I raced up the stairs I could hear Mrs. R. say something about what makes them crazy like that, and maybe they needed to be wormed.

I dashed into the Robertson's bedroom, across the carpet, and leaped to the window seat in a single bound. I was nothing, if not agile.

"Ofenm ouff thda vindah."

"What?" Watson was drooling. I told him that's what dogs do, but he never listens.

"Ofenm ouff thda vindah!" I repeated with more emphasis. It's darn hard to yell when you have a chicken leg in your mouth. And you're drooling.

"I can't understand you with that chicken leg in your mouth," Watson swallowed. "And you're drooling."

Very carefully, I pulled a tissue from the box on the dresser, and laid the leg down on it. "It would have helped greatly, if you had opened the window like I asked," I sighed.

"But I can't open the screen. And I didn't understand you with that chick- "

"Oh, stow it!" With claws extended, I worked the longest

one into the edge of the frame. A little wiggling and it slid back. I stuck my head out. "Hey! Kid!" I hissed.

A little head popped out from under the patio. "Yes, sir?"

"It's Purrlock, not Sir. Here. Catch this." I grabbed the chicken leg and tossed it out the window, careful not to get any grease on the cover of the window seat. No sense in leaving evidence. The chicken made a delicious squishing sound as it hit the ground. All those lovely juices....

The Kid sniffed it and meowed. The sound of a tiny tummy growling was almost as loud as the purring. "Is this all for me?"

"Yes. Now hide with it. Or we're all going to be in trouble."

"Thank you, Si...Purrlock." With a bit of effort, the furball got hold of the chicken leg and started dragging it across the lawn.

"Hey wait-- " No, maybe not. I was going to tell him to stay under the patio. But there was something about this little kid that bothered me. Another mystery, and we already had one on our plate. He disappeared behind the garage, as the rumbling of a doggy stomach reminded me our plates should have something on them.

"I'm starving. I could use an appetizer." The dog was such a weenie. Which I guess was logical, when you're built like one.

To this day, I don't know what made me do it. I could claim it was the devil, but somehow I don't think anyone would believe me. "Here," I pushed the tissue I'd laid the chicken on, over the edge of the dresser. "Eat that. It's roughage." And he did. The garbage disposal in the kitchen didn't work that fast.

"Didn't taste like roughage," he muttered as we made our way back down to the kitchen. "Tasted like chicken."

Chapter Nine

Could It Be...

Supper was in progress when we got to the kitchen, again. I headed straight for my custom-made, kitty shaped dish holder, with water on one side and...chow on the other. Chow? I was reduced to dry kibble? This was an outrage. This was animal cruelty. There was chicken on the table, and a cat on the floor. The two should be meeting and making beautiful chewing sounds. Actually, there were chewing sounds. Watson was slobbering through his bowl of dry chow. He never did have any standards.

I padded over to the table to sit beside Mrs. R. and lean against her leg. That's when I noticed something strange. I counted the feet under the table...one, two, three...four humans times two feet, makes eight. There were ten shoes here. I made my way to the middle of the forest of legs and sniffed. Those weren't Stevie's sneakers. His were wafting their usual 'odeur de garbage' from across the table. These were new. Hmmm, interesting. Watson blundered under Mr. R.'s chair and fell into Becca's legs.

"So," came a the headless voice of Mrs. R. somewhere up there where there was food, "How do you like living here, Andrew?"

Andrew! This was the #1 suspect for the silver thefts. I forgot begging, and slithered out to find a seat on the kitchen stool where I could see everyone, and listen to the conversation.

"It's okay," he shrugged.

"Play any sports?" Mr. R. wasn't much in the

communication department, but he could talk sports till the cows come home. Or that's what Mrs. R. said. And I was afraid sometimes when he got going, that they were going to show up at the back door.

"A little." Boy, the kid was short on words. "I like baseball, and sometimes soccer, but I'm not very good at either one."

I must say, he was a neat kid. That's to say he was clean as opposed to 'cool'. Stevie already had a pile of sopping wet napkins from spilling his milk, there was ketchup on his shirt, and when he tried to flip a french fry into his mouth, it left a red streak on his forehead. Andrew was neat as a pin. It was unnatural.

"Would you like some more rolls?" Mrs. R. held out the basket.

"No thanks." Andrew ducked his head and started picking at his chicken leg, again. I was willing to help him with that. Really, I was. Anything to be neighborly.

"Andrew-- " Stevie started to talk with a mouthful of cole slaw, then glanced over at Mrs. R. He closed it really quick, chewed and swallowed. "-- doesn't have any sisters." He stared at Becca across the table.

"You don't have any little brothers either, do you?" Becca smiled sweetly.

"Um," Andrew seemed a bit awkward and not sure if he was in the line of fire between the kids or not. "No. It's just Dad and me."

"You like computer games?" Mr. R. chimed in again. He was really trying. "I have all kinds of them, if you and your Dad would like to borrow some. I design software. What kind of work does your Dad do?"

"He's a veterinarian."

Arghhhhhhhhh. The dreaded "V" word. Needles, sharp things. I almost fell off my stool. We were harbouring a junior member of the Animal Chamber of Horrors.

"Watson, no begging at the table." Mrs. R. leaned over and caught the Big Boob reaching for a piece of chicken that Andrew was dangling. That dog had some cheek. The table was my territory.

"Sorry," Andrew mumbled and put the chicken back on his plate.

Mrs. R. glanced over at Mr. R. "How about some ice cream sundaes, everyone?"

"Not for me, thank you," Becca said primly. "I'm watching my figure."

"You're the only one," Stevie snickered. Just for a second, I thought I saw Andrew smile, but it was gone before Stevie yelled.

"Ow! She kicked me Mom!"

"Did not. I'm standing up, see?" Becca stood up, forgetting of course, that she had been sitting down when she kicked him. She sauntered out of the room, with the satisfied grin of someone who has scored a point.

"Sisters," snorted Stevie. "You're lucky you don't have any."

The adults were still drinking their coffee, when the boys got up. Andrew asked to be excused. "Of course," Mrs. R. smiled. After their chatter had faded down the hallway, she got up and started clearing the table.

"He seems like a nice boy, Edward. I find it really hard to believe that he's been taking things. Elaine Thompson told me his mother and father divorced, and she moved to out of State. He hasn't seen her in months."

Mr. R. was staring out the window. "I rebooted it first, I know I did."

"Edward," a note of exasperation was creeping into her voice. With any luck, she'd be distracted enough to forget the plate of leftover chicken was still on the cupboard. "The boy. I was talking about Andrew."

"What? I never booted Andrew." He looked bewildered. Which wasn't unusual.

Rats. She picked up the chicken platter and stood there with her other hand on her hip. I could reach it from the counter, but would never get away with it. Best to wait till it was unattended and lonely. Many chicken legs had found me good company. I welcomed them in with open jaws.

"I was saying that Andrew was a nice boy."

"Oh. Yes, he is. Stevie seems to like him. Maybe he just needs a little time to get used to a new house, and new people."

"As long as they're men," she said cryptically, setting the platter back down on the cupboard. Ah, my little lovelies. Come to Purrlock, you luscious little legs.

"Men." Mr. R. was really out of it. He had his coffee halfway to his mouth and I bet he couldn't remember if he was picking it up to drink, or was just setting it down."

"Yes, 'men'. Didn't you notice how he answered you, but I was lucky to get one word out of him at a time?" She shook her head. "It must have been very hard on him."

"What must?" Mr. R. looked in his coffee cup again, took a drink, and set it down.

"The divorce," she repeated. "Honestly, men!"

Mr. R. shoved his chair back and slunk quietly out of the room while her back was turned. He didn't know what he'd done wrong, but he didn't want to be told, either.

I was just a whisker's length from the chicken of my dreams when Mrs. R. caught me.

Chapter Ten

Purrlock to the Rescue

The boys were out in the backyard, with gloves and a baseball. Watson was watching them toss it back and forth, back and forth, back and forth… I could see him starting to weave. He was either dizzy or about to woof up his kibble.

"Hey, bone-breath" I called through the open kitchen window, where someone had thoughtfully built a new shelf for me to sit. After I had 'accidentally' clawed a set of curtains while falling into the sink. "Come over here and let me out."

"You're not allowed out," he woofed, never taking his eyes off the ball. Back and forth, back and forth….

"Am too, and you know it." Our backyard is all fenced in, but Mrs. R. won't let me out unless there is someone to watch and make sure I don't try to escape, or some desperate catnapper doesn't try to get in. The last time Watson made a remark about how desperate they'd have to be, we had a fight that got us both grounded.

I hated begging. But I was good at it. Jumping down off the window shelf, I brushed against Mrs. R.'s legs, meowed, purred, then went to the screen door and cried piteously.

"Oh for heaven's sake, couldn't you wait till I was done the dishes?" she scolded, while holding the door open. I gave her a last quick, ankle rub, and blinked my baby blue eyes at her. It worked every time. "You guys watch out for Purrlock, okay?"

47

"Sure Mom," Stevie called and side-armed the ball to Andrew.

"You're pretty good," Andrew brought it back and threw it to him again.

"Thanks." Stevie blushed just a little. He hated that, but at least Andrew didn't tease him about it. Becca would have been crowing for a week. "I went to baseball camp last summer. It helped a lot. Would you like to go this year? The coach at school can get you a form for your parents--I mean your Dad, to sign."

Andrew pulled his glove off and put it back on. "I dunno. I'll have to ask my Dad. He's really busy, and I don't know if he'd have the time."

"Gee, that's no problem. My Dad or Mom will pick us both up. It's great, really! There's lots of kids from all over town, and we have real experts in and everything."

Andrew threw him a perfect curveball. He wasn't such a bad pitcher himself. "I'll ask. It would be nice to have somewhere to go."

The ball went back and forth a few more times. "You have really cool pets," Andrew blurted. "Mom never let me have any. She said they were too much work."

"Naw," Stevie wound up and pitched again. "Purrlock is a real 'pussycat', and Watson is lots of fun. I let him sleep on my bed. But he can't get under the covers anymore. Well, just the blanket at the end of the bed. He farts something awful." Both of them started giggling like crazy. The dog pretended not to have heard. But I heard. And tucked the information away for future blackmail...er, use.

I had parked myself beside Watson, trying to get far enough away so his ears didn't smack me when he watched the ball, but close enough so we could talk without the humans thinking we were about to start a fight.

"He's not a very happy little boy," Watson observed. You

know, the dog wasn't totally stupid, after all. Very, very close sometimes. But then he had these flashes of brilliance.

"I know." My whiskers and ears were on the alert, swivelling, and testing. "Have you seen the Kid anywhere?" I glanced around, but cats can't see that far. And unless he moved, I wasn't going to be able to spot him. Much as I hated to, I was going to have to rely on the dog.

"Nope." With a shake of his head that got me an ear in the face, Watson flopped down on the grass and sighed. "Poor little guy. He's awfully lonely."

I stared at him. "You mean Andrew or the Kid?"

"I mean both," he replied. "Don't you think so?"

"Yeah," I agreed. Then I choked. I agreed with a dog. Next thing you know, I'd be snuggling with him for naps. Sure. When pigs fly. But he was right. The problem was-- how were we going to help either one of them?

Mr. R. came out of the house and went into the garage. He came back with a pair of grass clippers and began snipping along the fence and around the patio. I started to get up, but Watson put a paw over mine and shook his head just a tiny bit. His ears flapped over his own face this time. But I could tell that the Kid had pulled up stakes and was hiding elsewhere. I laid down in the grass beside the dog. Thank heavens for the fence and hedge, so nobody could actually see me doing this.

Mrs. R. came out and sat at the patio table with her cup of coffee. She was writing letters. Mr. R. was always after her to learn how to email. Then of course, she would ask him what good that would do when her mother, aunt, etc. etc. didn't have computers. You know, for a human she makes good sense now and then.

It was a warm evening, and even if I was full of dry chow instead of chicken, it was making me sleepy. I was about to slide down on top of the dog, who was already snoring, when Mrs. R's cell phone rang on the patio.

"Hello? Yes, Marjorie, it's me. No. No, I haven't heard anything. What?"

I hated hearing one side of a conversation. Not that I eaves drop, but you never know when they're making you an appointment with the vet.

"I don't believe it! Another one? How did they manage it? When? Yes, I see. Well, I know for certain one suspect they can eliminate." Mrs. R. glanced down the yard to where the boys were just coming up to the patio, swinging their gloves and talking about how much they hated math class.

"Yes, thank you. I will." Mrs. R. hung up the phone and called Mr. R. over to the railing.

"There's been another theft, Edward. This time it was Harvey Garland's keychain with that little silver dog whistle on it."

"Oh good," I heard the mutt mumble. "That thing sure hurts the ears."

Mr. R. stood there snapping his shears, as if they could cut through the mystery of the missing goods. "A key chain? Stolen?" he mused.

They weren't paying attention to the boys. Suddenly Andrew yelled "I didn't take it! I didn't!" His face turned red, he threw his glove on the ground and ran down the yard, disappearing behind the garage.

"Oh dear," Mrs. R. came running down the stairs. "You can be sure it wasn't him, because it was just taken, not ten minutes ago, off the picnic table in their yard."

The humans all ran down the lawn after Andrew, with Watson flopping behind, and me on his tail. The gate in the fence was swinging, but there was no sign of Andrew anywhere.

"He didn't do it, Mom. Honest. And he didn't take any of the other things, either." Stevie looked down at his shoes, then up at Mrs. R. "I just know he didn't."

"I know too." She put an arm around his shoulders and turned back towards the house. "I think we should go in and call his father. He had better hear about this from us, because if it comes to the question of where he was, we all know that Andrew had nothing to do with it."

If it hadn't been for that dog's ears, they never would have found the Kid. Watson started forward, tripped over himself, and landed with a 'whump' in the grass.

Unfortunately, the whump did not drown out the tiny hiss.

"Why, Edward...look!" Mrs. R. bent down and in the grass at the bottom of the garage wall, picked up our fugitive furball. "It's a tiny kitten. Oh my word, isn't he sweet?"

I'd have gagged, but I was too busy winding myself around their feet, hoping they'd put him down, so we could stash him away again. He was kicking and squirming and hollering at us, although the humans couldn't understand him. It didn't help that Watson was barking, although to give him credit, he was trying to reassure the Kid that he was safe with *our* humans.

"Help me! Help me! Make them put me down. I don't want to go. Don't let them take me away!"

"Shoo, Purrlock. Out from under my feet." Mrs. R. cuddled the little....brat to her chest. "He's scared of you big, noisy animals." And with that she scooted off into the house, trailed by Mr. R. with his shears, and Stevie with a hopeful look.

"Can we keep him, Mom?"

Keep him? KEEP him? I didn't bargain on this when I gave him that chicken. Invite him over for dinner and he takes over my humans. And my home. Even my dog!

"Let's not get ahead of ourselves," she said firmly, setting the Invader on the floor. "I've got to go call Andrew's father. Maybe he'll come over and look at the kitten. It's really too small to have left its mother, and he's very thin. Stevie, you go get one of those aluminium pans, and some of Purrlock's litter. Then I'll put some water down for him, and a little chopped chicken. Then we'll leave him here in the kitchen and shut the door. I think maybe we're scaring him."

Well, she was right about that. The Kid was scrunched on the floor, shaking like last night's Jello. His eyes were so big, they took up most of his face. He'd stopped meowing and kept darting looks around the room. I could have told him about the dog door, but considering he was about to get my chicken, I figured he could wait.

We were all shooed out, Mr. R. back to his yard work, Stevie, Watson and I, out to the hallway. Stevie ran upstairs to tell Becca about "our" new kitten.

I sat outside the door and thought. The dog sat there and stared off into space. I smacked him one upside the head, and he yipped.

"Earth to Watson. Beam down here Bozo, and open that kitchen door for me." It was one of those swinging doors, but you had to have some weight behind it, and fluffy old me, just wasn't enough.

"You just want his chicken." the dog glared.

"If I wanted chicken, I'd get it. I want to talk to the Kid. And we better hurry because she's not going to be on that phone all night."

"Well, alright," he nosed the door open. "But he needs it

more than you do."

I ignored the Basset beast and trotted over to where the Kid was huddled at the screen door.

"Can you let me out, please?" When he turned towards us, there were tiny tears on his face. He hadn't even touched the chicken.

"In a minute," I said, sitting down. "Let's have a little chat, first."

"But I need to go. I really, really do. Please let me out." I hated pleading and begging. Unless it was the dog, when I had him by the ear.

"Look, Kid...I know you're hiding something, and I don't think it's that chicken leg I threw you. You stumbled around explaining how you got left alone by your humans, then when I tossed that leg out, you dragged it off and hid, instead of staying where you were safe, and eating it." He was inching away from me and towards Watson. I gave the dog a warning 'look', not to butt in.

"It doesn't take Sherlock, or even Purrlock Holmes to figure out that you didn't leave that house alone. Did you?" I leaned over him, in the old 'intimidate' mode again. Whatever he was hiding, we needed to know...now.

"No." He sniffed, and another tear rolled down his nose. Watson reached over and licked his face. Ewwwww. But effective. "Thank you," he wiped a paw over the sopping wet fur of his face. "My sister is out there behind the garage. Under the floor at the back. She's smaller than me, and she's really scared. I took the chicken leg out to her, and we shared it. She won't come out, because she's afraid. A big dog almost caught her yesterday, and now she won't come out at all, and I can't leave her there by herself."

"No problem," I patted him on the head. "Open the door, and let's go." I nudged the dog.

"Eh? What?" Watson started up and would have tripped over his ears again if I hadn't held them up while the three of us snuck out the doggie door.

Chapter Eleven

Out on a Limb

The Kid led us across the lawn to the garage. "I dunno," Watson muttered. "We are in BIG trouble with capital letters, if they find us. Not only are you out, he's out too and I'll get the blame."

"That's because you let us out." Why cheer him up now? I had been nice to him all day. Well, almost.

"Nooooo!" the Kid screamed and leaped around the corner.

There was Andrew, sitting with his back against the garage wall, and a little calico kitten in his lap. Andrew's face was dirty, and I could tell he'd been crying. But he was smiling a little bit now.

"Hey there, little guy." He picked up the Kid and put him beside the other kitten. "Do you two know each other?"

They sure did. The Kid nuzzled his sister, and licked her, then she blinked and started purring. I could hear Watson sniffling. Geez, that dog was such a softie.

"I'll bet you're brother and sister," Andrew stroked their fur gently, as they cuddled together in his lap. "I can tell she's a girl because of her colour. My Dad taught me all about that. It's called genetics, and that's how you figure out what colour kittens are going to be." He was talking more to Watson and I, than he'd talked to the Robertsons.

I sidled up and nosed the Kid. Watson laid his head on

Andrew's leg. Andrew reached a hand out to each of us for a pat.

"Purrlock Holmes!" Ruh-roh. We were caught.

"Hi," Andrew looked up at Mrs. R. then down at the kittens in his lap. I could tell he figured he was in trouble with us.

"You bad boy." Ack. I was swooped up in her arms and forced to submit to kissing…in front of the dog. "How did you get out here?"

"I think he probably came out with Watson." Andrew scratched the dog under his chin. He was smirking, and the best I could do was glare a promise of revenge.

"Well, we're going to have to put a stop to that. What have you got there?" When he patted the dog, Mrs. R. got a glimpse of the tiny furballs. "Why, that's our kitten. They let him out, too!"

"Really?" Andrew held the little calico out for her to see. "I found her under the garage in that hollow. I--I hid around the side when you all came looking for me." Down went the head, again.

"Oh, Andrew. Did you really think we believed you had taken those things?"

He shrugged and kept his head down, stroking the furry little bodies. "The kids at school say their parents all believe it was me. Because I was in all those houses. But I didn't do it. Honest."

When he finally raised his face there were streaks of dirt, where he'd rubbed his hands over his eyes.

"We know that," Mrs. R. said firmly, holding out a hand to him, and leaving me hanging over the other arm. "Now come on up to the house. We have to let your father know where you are. And he's going to come over and see one kitten, so maybe he can look at two."

They walked up the lawn together, Andrew cradling the kittens, me draped over Mrs. R.'s shoulder, and Watson following behind, with his tongue stuck out. Yes, I know dogs pant and let their tongues hang. But this time he stuck it out. I swear he did. Honest!

The only compensation for the indignity of being dragged in like this, was the view. From up here I got a close-up of the clothesline, the birdhouse on a pole, and a crow that kept swooping over our heads. Things were turning out pretty good. Out...out....why did that word make my whiskers stand on end?

In the kitchen, Andrew set the kittens down on the floor, and Becca joined them, making coo-coo noises. I can't help it. I glared at them. That was, after all, my human. I rushed over and plopped myself in her lap, rolling over on my back. "Around here, we share, kids."

"Okay." They rubbed up against me and crawled into my belly fur.

"Awwwwww." Geesh, humans were such soft touches.

The little girl kitten meowed softly and started purring as the Kid licked her all over. Boy, they could make a lot of noise for two little kids. Oh shoot...that noise was me. I was purring, too. Until Becca dumped me unceremoniously on the floor and the dog started snickering.

"Are we going to keep them, Mom? Please?"

"Yeah Mom, please? Pretty please?" Stevie came into the kitchen ahead of Mr. R. and Andrew's father.

While they were busy putting me out of house and home, and forgetting who taught them the joys of being owned by a cat, I bit Watson on the tail to get his attention.

"The door. Hurry." I hissed, slapping a paw over his muzzle before he yelped.

"Mmmat huft," he whimpered, slinking over to the doggie door and cautiously pushing the flap open. "That hurt!" he repeated when we made it out to the patio, unnoticed.

"Sorry, but I wanted to get away before they stopped talking about replacing me with one of those furry little traitors."

"Oh, I don't think they'd-- "

"Quiet." I swatted him on the ear. "I need to think." And I have to admit, I was just the tiniest bit out of sorts at the idea of having to share my catnip mice.

"But I wish they would, sometimes." Watson muttered, flopping down on the grass under the big maple tree.

"Out. Out. Why does 'out' mean something to me?"

"Because you're not allowed there. Here. Out, I mean." He snuffled his nose into the grass and got an ant up one nostril. I'd have laughed, but my mind was on other things.

"Out. All the things that were stolen were outside! Or they could be reached from outside!" I grabbed Watson's ears and yanked on them. Okay, I was excited and maybe pulled a little too hard.

He jumped up and growled. "I have had enough of you and your--"

"Think, think." I patted his head encouragingly. "Mrs. Perry's earrings were on the patio table. A window in Mr. Mittlejohn's study was open, but it was way up off the ground. Then the screen was out of Mr. Greenberg's porch. And Mrs. Thompson dropped her chain out side the porky Persian's pen."

Watson wrinkled his brow and sat down again. "But couldn't someone have walked in through the door?"

"Sure, but not with people in the house. Mr. Greenberg was home. The Perry's kids where in the house with Pascal. They were taken by someone who could get in and out, without going through a door."

"Yeah! You're right." He sat up and looked at me expectantly. "So who was it?"

You know, on those late shows Mr. R. watches, there is always a big drum roll or some really dramatic music for a moment like this.

"It was...him!" I jumped into the air, even though I missed the crow by a good ten feet. His raucous laughter really irritated me, too.

"Ha-ha-ha, you overstuffed hairball. What are you gonna do about it, huh?"

"The crow?" Watson stared, dumbfounded. We found him dumb a lot of the time.

"Yes. Remember that time Mrs. R. was watching the National Geographic special on bird life, and she thought it was so cute when I chased the birds on the screen?"

The crow streaked down out of the tree and skimmed over my back. I dropped my tail as he grabbed for the fur. "Watch it you thief!" I screamed as he did a circuit of the yard and came in for another dive.

"Yes, that was so disgusting. You left pawprints on the screen," the dog sniffed.

"At least they wiped off your nose prints," I snarled back. The crow took another shot at me and I flattened myself into the grass. "If you'd been watching the screen instead of snoozing, you'd have seen them show how crows will steal anything that is *shiny*. Silver is shiny. What's bets that he's got that stuff up there in the tree? And he just admitted as much."

"Carrrggghhhh!" cackling with glee, the crow dove in again, and this time I jumped aside, leaving the dog unprotected. He grabbed Watson by the ear, yanking it over his face and scaring him so bad, he fell over and lay there howling.

"Ow! Ow! I can't see. Help me! Help me!"

I flipped the ear off his face before making another leap for the crow. "That's it! That's my dog. Nobody touches my dog but me." And off I raced, right up the tree and along the big bottom branch, before I knew what kind of stupid thing I'd done. Way up there…and the ground way down there.

"So whatcha want, Furry And Fat?" The crow sidled along the branch, daring me to follow him.

"I want those things back. They aren't yours. And people think that Andrew took them." I snarled and lashed my tail. Well, it always worked on Watson. But it didn't seem to ruffle any crow feathers.

"Well la-di-da-da. Like I should care? They're shiny and I like them. Finders keepers, fat cats are the weepers."

Ooh, that hurt. That really hurt. So I did another stupid thing. I made a big leap toward him into the leaves, and discovered the widest part of the branch ended about half a leap behind me. I fell through some leaves and was left hanging by my claws from a branch about the width of Watson's tail. The crow flew off, flapping his beak about coming back to get what was his.

For once I was grateful for the yapping dog. His frenzied barking had brought every one out of the house, and they were all under the tree, calling and yelling. At me. Yell at the crow, why don't you? And get me down out of here!

"Oh, Edward!" Mrs. R. cried. I knew that voice. She was going to cry for real if someone didn't get me down. And I might just join her. "He's right out at the end. And it's such a little branch."

"But he's a cat, dear." Mr. R. was really a soft touch, when he was in touch with the rest of the world. "He'll find his way down."

"When was the last time you saw Purrlock up a tree?" she demanded.

"Well, actually...um, never." He looked up. I'd rather he hurried up and did something. "I'll get the ladder."

"Let me," Andrew's father volunteered. "I'm smaller and lighter. I won't put as much weight against the largest branch, and maybe I can reach over to grab him."

Come on, folks. My claws only have so many hours of staying power in them. Let's get a move on.

I was casting around for a place to grab onto as my paws started slipping, when I spotted the crow's nest. And hanging over the side was a shiny, silver chain.

"Hi there, Purrlock. Are you scared up here?" The soft voice was Mr. Scott, Andrew's father. He was reaching out a hand to me, but it was too far away.

Hating myself for it, I bawled "Yeowwww!" and swung on the branch, until it shook and the leaves pulled away from the crow's nest. I could hear Becca crying, Mrs. R. sniffling, and the dog whimpering.

"That's okay, we'll get you down. Just hang on a little bit longer." He was a nice man, I could tell. But did he really think I was ready to let go? Geesh.

As Mr. Scott held onto the large branch with one arm, he leaned over the side of the ladder and reached for me.

"Look dear," I heard Mr. R. say, as casually as if he saw this kind of thing every day, "there's a silver chain hanging out of that nest."

I lost track of his musings at that point, as a hand grabbed me by the scruff and hauled me across the Chasm of Death and put me over a warm shoulder. "There we go," Mr. Scott soothed, patted, and talked, instead of getting down off the gently waving ladder, perched against a branch that creaked and groaned. I think I'm going to like him a lot. But I'd like him a lot better on the ground.

With Stevie and Andrew steadying the ladder, he backed down cautiously, and handed me over to Mrs. R. I was then forced to endure kissing and hugging and tears in my fur, and I loved every second of it. But I will never admit it.

While we had a family reunion, Mr. R. and Andrew's father moved the ladder to a safer spot where they could get at the crow's nest. Mr. Scott went back up, and came down with a pocketful of treasure.

"Let's take everyone back into the house," he smiled at Andrew. "I think maybe we can make some phone calls and return a few things after. How about that, son?"

"Yeah, that would be great." Andrew smiled.

On the kitchen table, they laid out the treasures of the crow's nest. I wiggled out of Mrs. R.'s clutches, until she let me down. On the most forbidden of places--the table.

"It's all there," she marvelled.

"Plus some," Mr. Scott laughed. "The earrings, lighter, silver dollar, chain, the whistle, two dimes, a ball bearing, and some penny nails. He's been a busy bird."

I was investigating the recovered loot, touching the whistle with a paw, when I heard Watson from below the table.

"Can't you eat that one, or something?" he moaned.

"I can't see."

"Me either," came a second tiny voice. The kids were trying to crawl up Andrew's leg.

He bent over and cupping one in each hand, brought them together.

"See? That's what Purrlock found when he chased the bird. And now everyone will know it wasn't me. I really enjoyed doing errands for people, and now I'll need the money." He smiled as the kittens snuggled closer.

"That's right," his father agreed. "They're going to need vaccinations, and then they need to be altered, and there's food and litter beside. You're lucky you've got a vet in the family. I might just give you a discount if you keep the lawn mowed and the garden weeded."

"Sure!"

Becca reached around him to pat the Kid. "I'd still like another cat, but I don't mind that Andrew has these two. I know he's going to take care of them."

I stared at her. Pah. Traitor! This is what I get for keeping her feet warm at night? I would have to consider where to hack my next hairball.

"And we still have Purrlock." She swept me off the table,

and hugged me till I gurgled for mercy. It was nice to be loved. I could hear the dog gagging, he was so moved.

"What are you going to name them?" Stevie asked as they moved towards the hallway.

"I don't know," Andrew thought for a minute. "Something special, though."

Mrs. R. looked at me, then back at the kid. "Well, you know Sherlock Holmes had a brother named 'Mycroft'."

"But he didn't have a sister." Stevie elbowed Becca.

"Mommmmm!"

The noise died away, as the humans walked to the front door.

I jumped down off the table, and started an intimate inspection of the dog's ear.

"What are you doing?" he asked suspiciously.

"Checking for beak marks," I mumbled. Was that one? I licked it just in case, smoothing down the fur. Then I licked a little more. He'd had a hard day.

With a sigh, Watson collapsed in a heap on the floor. I was a little tired myself. 'I'll sit, just for a minute,' I thought. Maybe laying would be better. I don't know how it happened, but I was stretched out against a warm dog and purring. That's when the world exploded in light.

Mrs. R. stood in the kitchen door, laughing.

"She got new batteries for the camera," I explained to the dozy dog. And now she'd gotten a picture. I was never going to live this down. Never.

Letters to the Editor

Dear Editor:

I just wanted you to know, that I thought it was real nice of you to make a book about my friends, Purrlock and Watson.

They are pretty good company, and always try to be nice to the rest of us in the neighborhood. I like it when they come to visit, because then I get to hear all the news from up and down the street.

Your friend,
Pascal
The Giant Schnauzer

Dear Pascal:

Thank you so much for writing us. We enjoyed the book, too. It was a little hard to believe that a cat and dog that get on each other's nerves that much, can actually be friends. But it appears that they are both a pair of big softies.
The Editors
(Note: The galley proof of this page was found with the comment "AM NOT!" scrawled on it.)

Dear Editor:

I am having my friend the parrot, write this, as it's very hard to hold a pen in your fins. And not many of them will write underwater.

It's about the cat. Not that he hasn't been helpful and everything, but he makes me nervous. Every time he looks at me, I see fish 'n chips in his eyes.

Anyway, I just wanted you to know, that if I don't appear in the next book, you should check the cat for scales on his whiskers.

Bubblingly yours,
Goldie
The Fish

Dear Goldie:

Thank you so much for the note. We don't think you really need to worry about Purrlock too much. He's much more of a pussycat, than he seems.
We're sure that the way he looks at you, is just his way of having a little fun.
The Editors
(Note: Galley proof of this page also found with "AM NOT!" scrawled on it. Check with printers.)

Dear Editor:

You got something against turtles? How come I didn't get a bigger part? They'd never have caught on to how only silver things were stolen, if I hadn't told them about the coin.

And what did I get out of it? One lousy worm. It was tough, too.

I want my picture on the cover, and 20% of the royalties. And a plate of worms.

One ticked off turtle,
Calvin

Dear Calvin:

We are sorry that you did not come off better in the book. But we can only print what Purrlock wrote.
Not that we're positive about this, but we think the crack about the hamster, may have had something to do with it.
The Editors
(Note: Galley proof had "Darn right" written on it. Call security about access to offices.)

Listen up, whoever you are:

I have had enough of that fruitcake furball and his dumbbell sidekick. They have insulted me for the last time.

I will have my revenge, and it won't be pretty.

One more word off your presses that is less than absolute adoration, complimenting my beautiful fur, my stunning green eyes, or my lithe and oh so graceful body, and I will shred every piece of paper in your offices, including the twaddle written by that twit, whats-his-name.

And I mean business.

No name,
You Know Who This Is

Dear You Know:
"Sticks and stones may break bones", but not yours Beefy. Nobody can find them through the fat.
(Note: Install new security system and then find out who added this reply.)

Dear Mr. Editor:

Purrlock has taught us how to use the computer, so I thought I would write you a letter.

Thanks to Purrlock, my sister and I have a new home, with lots of food and love, and we never have to go outside where it's dangerous, and we can get chased by dogs or scared by cars.

Our people didn't want us I guess. We were lost and all by ourselves, with nowhere to go. But Andrew took us home! We are so happy that we will have a place to live forever, and ever.

With purrs and headbutts,
Mycroft and Millicent Scott

Dear Mycroft and Millicent:

We are very happy too, because every year, thousands of beautiful little cats like you, also find themselves without a home. That's why it is important for everyone to spay and neuter their pets.
The Editors

Visit

www.purrlockholmes.com

Read reviews of this book, and add your own!

Find out about the "real" Purrlock Holmes!

Learn what goes into writing a book!

and lots more!!!

Write Purrlock himself: Purrlock@purrlockholmes.com

Write Watson: Watson@purrlockholmes.com

Write the author, Betty Sleep
author@purrlockholmes.com

LaVergne, TN USA
22 November 2009

164957LV00004B/172/P